New York (State) Legislature

Proceedings of the Senate and Assembly of the State of New York

on the life and character of James Gillespie Blaine

New York (State) Legislature

Proceedings of the Senate and Assembly of the State of New York
on the life and character of James Gillespie Blaine

ISBN/EAN: 9783337093549

Printed in Europe, USA, Canada, Australia, Japan

Cover: Foto ©Raphael Reischuk / pixelio.de

More available books at **www.hansebooks.com**

In Memoriam.

James Gillespie Blaine.

" In halls of state he stood for many years,
Like fabled knight his visage all aglow,
Receiving, giving sternly, blow for blow."

" The gap this breach hath left is wide,
The loss thereof can never be supplied."

PROCEEDINGS

OF THE

SENATE AND ASSEMBLY

OF THE

STATE OF NEW YORK,

ON THE LIFE AND CHARACTER OF

JAMES GILLESPIE BLAINE.

Albany, February 13, 1893.

ALBANY:

JAMES B. LYON, STATE PRINTER.

1893.

PROCEEDINGS

OF THE

SENATE AND ASSEMBLY

OF THE

STATE OF NEW YORK,

ON THE LIFE AND CHARACTER OF

JAMES GILLESPIE BLAINE.

Albany, February 13, 1893.

ALBANY:

JAMES B. LYON, STATE PRINTER.

1893.

JOINT COMMITTEE OF THE LEGISLATURE.

ON THE PART OF THE SENATE.

GEORGE F. ROESCH,   CLARENCE E. BLOODGOOD,

CHARLES T. SAXTON.

ON THE PART OF THE ASSEMBLY.

JAMES H. SOUTHWORTH,   JOHN A. HENNESSY,

ALFRED HENNEN MORRIS,   JAMES TERRY,

JOHN M. DIVEN.

PROCEEDINGS

OF THE

LEGISLATURE OF THE STATE OF NEW YORK

RELATIVE TO THE

LIFE AND SERVICES

OF

JAMES GILLESPIE BLAINE.

PROCEEDINGS OF THE SENATE.

IN SENATE, *January* 27, 1893.

Mr. CANTOR offered the following:

Resolved (if the Assembly concur), That a joint committee, consisting of three Senators and five Members of Assembly, be appointed by the respective presiding officers of the two Houses, for the purpose of presenting resolutions in memory of the deceased statesman, James G. Blaine.

The PRESIDENT put the question whether the Senate would agree to said resolution, and it was decided in the affirmative.

Out of respect to the memory of James G. Blaine, Senator CANTOR moved that the Senate adjourn until Monday evening at 8.30.

The PRESIDENT put the question whether the Senate would agree to said motion, and it was decided in the affirmative.

Whereupon the Senate adjourned.

JANUARY 31, 1893.

The Assembly returned the concurrent resolution relative to the appointment of a joint committee to draft resolutions in memory of James G. Blaine, with a message that they have concurred in the passage of the same.

In Memoriam.

FEBRUARY 1, 1893.

The PRESIDENT appointed Messrs. Roesch, Bloodgood and Saxton as the committee on the part of the Senate, to draft suitable resolutions relative to the death of James G. Blaine.

FEBRUARY 13, 1893.

Mr. SAXTON, on behalf of the joint committee of the Senate and Assembly, to draft suitable resolutions appropriate to the death of James G. Blaine, presented the following on behalf of the Senate:

WHEREAS, By the death of James Gillespie Blaine, this country has lost one of her most illustrious sons, a a brilliant historian, an eloquent orator, a matchless debater, and accomplished publicist, a great and renowned statesman, one whose genius has left an indelible impress for good upon our political life and national policies; one whose fame, leaping beyond the borders of his own land, has spread through all civilized nations; one who loved his country with the fervent love of the true patriot, and who had a warmer place in the hearts of the American people than any other man of his time.

Resolved, That this Senate give public expression to the profound sense of loss felt at this time by all classes of his fellow citizens in the Empire State; their gratitude for his priceless services; their sorrow for his death and respect for his memory.

Resolved, That these resolutions, with the preamble, be spread on the journal of the Senate, and an engrossed copy of the same forwarded to his bereaved family, with the assurance of the deep sympathy felt for them by the individual members of this body.

In moving the adoption of the foregoing resolutions, Mr. SAXTON spoke as follows:

Mr. PRESIDENT.—The career of James G. Blaine was one of the most interesting and remarkable in our

10

James Gillespie Blaine.

political history. His official life commenced in 1853, when he was elected to the lower House of the Maine Legislature. He served four years in that body, twice as its presiding officer. In 1862 he became a representative in Congress from one of the Maine districts, and for fourteen years, I think, the House of Representatives was the arena for the exercise of his extraordinary talents. Three times he was chosen Speaker of the House, and afterward leader of the Republican minority. In 1876 he lacked but a few voters for the presidential nomination by the Republican National Convention. Soon after, he entered the Senate of the United States, from which he retired to accept the portfolio of State in President Garfield's Cabinet. In 1884 he became the standard-bearer of the Republican party in the national campaign of that year, but although he made a gallant and splendid fight he was defeated. Like other of our greatest men he was destined never to grasp the glittering prize of the presidency. Doubtless, he felt at times, as all have felt in hours of failure, "the emptiness of all things, from politics to pastimes," but no personal disaster had power to break his spirit or weaken his love and loyalty for his native land.

His last public position was that of Secretary of State in the present administration, and his brilliant course during the three years that he filled that great office not only added brighter luster to his fame, but gained him the respect and admiration even of his political adversaries. In the earlier part of his career he may have been too much of the mere politician, but time and experience had ripened him into the

11

firm, sagacious, broad-minded, far-sighted, progressive and patriotic statesman. His pan-American policy was the consummation of his political life, and proved to all that his genius for statecraft was of the very highest order. The new world is the home of republics as the old world is of monarchies. Believing that the destinies of America should not be controlled by the political formulas of Europe, but should be fixed by the laws of her own growth and development, he grasped the idea of binding together the nations of the western hemisphere by bonds of friendship and mutual interest; and then put his conception into practical form by inaugurating a movement that must result in establishing the most cordial relations between this country and her sister republics.

What would the history of our recent politics be without James G. Blaine? Every page is illuminated with the flashings of his master intellect. Every question he touched with the magic of his genius sprang into new and glowing life. No matter what he did he always produced the effect of a bit of vivid color in a somewhat somber and monotonous landscape. He was the center of every political movement. All eyes were turned toward him, some with a sympathetic interest that never waned, and others reluctantly, as if drawn by a power of fascination they could not resist.

At the time of his death he was by common consent the most illustrious of our public men. We were accustomed to regard him as the foremost of American citizens, a title which is a prouder decoration than a scepter or a crown. Thoroughly American in every fiber of his being, his ambition was to enhance the glory and promote the prosperity of the American republic. While he was, as will generally be conceded, the greatest statesman of the *post bellum* period, he was also pre-eminent as a historian, a parliamentarian, an orator and a diplomat.

But we think of him most frequently as a popular leader. With a charming personality, a wonderful power of strong and luminous statement, a dashing, chivalric spirit that excited the imagination, and a daring that sometimes bordered upon audacity, it is no wonder that the "Plumed Knight" was the idol of his own party, or that he was able to wring from his opponents the tribute of unwilling praise. He was unquestionably the most popular man of his time, and I doubt if any American statesman ever enjoyed, during his lifetime, so great a share of popular favor as did James G. Blaine. He had, in a notable degree, that quality which we call magnetism. Wherever he went he was received with an enthusiasm which no other man could awaken. He seemed to attach men to him, and hold them by the strongest of all ties, that of personal affection. Through all the vicissitudes of his long political life the plain people always loved him and trusted him and sympathized with him. Their affection for him sometimes seemed blind and unreasoning, but it had both its reason and justification, for his heart went out to them in return and he seemed instinctively to divine the needs and express the ideals of the great mass of his fellow citizens. They deeply mourn his death and will fondly cherish his memory.

To my mind James G. Blaine was the greatest figure in this country, with one or two possible exceptions,

during the last twenty-five years; and leaving out of
the account those distinguished generals of our civil
war who have been crowned with military laurels, his
fame will rise higher and rest upon a firmer foundation
than that of any American of this generation except
the immortal Lincoln. Posterity will rank him with
the greatest men of the century, and his name will be
written in letters of sparkling light upon the pages of
history.

By Senator Roesch:

Mr. President.—The Republic sustained a severe loss
in the death of James G. Blaine. Around his grave
party strife is hushed and the malignity of political
slander is silenced in the praise of the dead. His
true position in the American Walhalla can not
yet be awarded him. His death is too recent
and his works have not met with that fruition
which their author presaged for them. We may
have differed seriously in his lifetime as to the
policy of his ambitions and may have conscien-
tiously criticised the methods adopted to assure
their accomplishment, yet no one will deny the magnificent Americanism of the man and no one can deny
his pre-eminent qualifications for the various public
stations he filled. He came from Revolutionary stock.
His grandfather was an officer in the Revolutionary
War and a friend of George Washington. He could
thus trace a proud lineage of American ancestors
from whom he inherited his intense love for America
and her interests. While at college he was a leader
in his studies as well as in its athletic sports and

he thus produced that grand physical presence which in after life was the delight of multitudes of his fellow countrymen. He led too in the debating society, that peculiar American institution which can lay claim to the early cultivation of those powers which saw their noblest development on the rostrum and in the halls of legislation. He was a ready and an apt scholar; enjoyed great personal popularity among his associates and was frequently made the arbitrator in their youthful disputes. Thus did the boy truly foreshadow the man. As a professor in a western military college he won rank as an educator. It is impossible now to follow him in all the details of his brilliant career but some of them might be briefly and rapidly sketched. As an editor he molded and shaped public opinion in his locality and was a bold and fearless critic. He was one of the organizers of the Republican party of Maine in 1856 and an active Member of the Legislature of his adopted State. As a Member of Congress and thrice Speaker of the House of Representatives he was the foremost parliamentarian of the age, a dangerous adversary in debate, a bitter and relentless supporter of party measures. He was right. Our government is one of party and the sturdy exchange of party views and intelligent and honest discharge of public duties will produce the noblest type of American public men. The friends of constitutional liberty throughout the land do not forget the signal, though indirect, service James G. Blaine rendered to the great commoner, Samuel J. Randall, in his efforts to defeat the Force Bill by fillibustering when the

former was Speaker of the House. He aided in the
defeat of that measure because he held that the
remedy for alleged southern troubles should come
from the southern people themselves and thus again
demonstrated his unbounded faith in the healthy
public sentiment of American communities. Nor do
the friends of constitutional government forget that
as United States Senator James G. Blaine voted
against that makeshift for political justice, the electoral commission bill, which like every other political
compromise was the fruitful parent of fraud. He was
always in advance of his party in political thought,
and for that reason was the bright target for the shafts
not of the opposition alone but of his own political
household as well. He denounced the measure of economic reform upon which his party staked its success in
the last political campaign as one which did not open a
market in the world for our products, and he did not
desist until a provision was adopted whereby important
trade concessions could be demanded from other countries
in return for the removal of impost duties upon com-
modities, and thus secured legislative recognition of his
doctrine of reciprocal trade relations. He was a man
of most versatile mind. When he entered the Senate
he was not expected to take part in any but political debates, yet when the question of the Geneva award
was under consideration he delivered an argument so
strictly legal in its tone and exhaustive of the legal and
equitable rights involved under the laws of our country
and the law of nations, that it won commendation from
a great leader of the American bar and bright particular
star of the United States Senate, the late Matt H. Car-

penter. The Pan-American Congress was a grand conception though it did not work out its important fullness. The nations of the earth to-day more than ever recognize the spirit of its calling, and the headlong rush into the horrors of war is now only a treat of ancient history. All mankind pays homage to the doctrine of peace and arbitration in the family relations of the nations of the earth, and James G. Blaine deserves a large measure of credit for the presence of the angel of peace. Mr. President, I repeat that the republic has sustained a great loss in the death of James G. Blaine. We may not yet be able to allot to him his proper sphere in history Party feeling may yet run too high to allow deliberate, cool and dispassionate judgment to give him that credit for his works in our national life which he so thoroughly deserved. Yet thousands not of his political faith will acknowledge the grand characteristics of the man, and to the younger men of our generation James G. Blaine stands out in American history as the grand type of American manhood after which all American youth of the land may well pattern.

By Senator O'Connor :

Mr. President.— I cannot let the present opportunity pass without paying my humble tribute to the great commoner who is the subject of these resolutions. In the very recent conflict, I had the honor to work zealously, hoping to bring about his nomination as the standard bearer of the Republican party, believing him to be the greatest man of the present generation.

No man who has been an observer of current history of American politics for the past thirty years, can fail to be impressed with the great services that James G. Blaine has rendered his country and his fellow citizens. In 1862, he first came into the arena of national politics by being elected a Member of Congress, at a time when the nation was engaged in the throes of civil conflict and its life trembling in the balance. He brought to the solution of the great questions that were then propounded to the American people his brilliant intellectual attainments and superior genius. In every strife from that time until death fixed his eyes in eternal sleep, he was a conspicuous, if not the most conspicuous personality in American politics. On every question which concerned the honor of his country, or of his fellow citizens, any man who studies his career, must render to him the tribute at all times of having been animated by the most patriotic and unselfish purposes.

Mr. Blaine was an intellectual giant among men. He foresaw results with a Napoleonic precision, and he had the intelligence and genius to grasp opportunities and instruments that were best calculated and fitted to attain these results. In these thirty years the nature and scope of our national government has been changed, or if not changed, at least molded into such permanent shape that its character is as fixed and everlasting as the hills. We have seen the extreme doctrine of State rights disappear; we have seen demonstrated as the result of his labor and the labors of other men animated by the same patriotic motives that the stars and stripes represent a nation and not a confederacy of States; that this nation is a chain of indestructible steel, and not a rope of sand; that in the face of any and all emergencies it possesses the inherent power to preserve its life without

---

doing violence to the rights of States or to the liberties of individuals.

On every question arising out of that strife the American people have had the benefit of Mr. Blaine's genius and his patriotism. But there came a period in his career when the praise of a portion of the people was turned to censure. Mr. Blaine believed that the citizen who best loved his party and was loyal to it was loyal to and best loved his country. He despised Phariseeism and cant. He recognized in national politics no place for the Mugwumps or the so-called Independents; the men who pursued a guerilla warfare in public life, ever ready to make terms with the party that offered them the greatest inducements, and when they received their price and fixed their abode, seek to dominate and control the power and policy of that party. These were the men whose praise was turned into censure and whose venemous attack on Mr. Blaine was a disgrace to our people and civilization.

If there is anything for which James G. Blaine deserves the admiration of the American people it is for his magnificent courage in pressing every problem with an honest and thorough conviction and belief that what he advocated was for the best interest of the people.

I believe the true secret of the attack on his personal character is due to the fact that he wrote a book which in the future generations will be quoted as are "Cæsar's Commentaries." His "Twenty Years in Congress" is but a name. It is not as much his career in Congress as it is the history of the country during its most important epoch. Therein he disclosed his intense Americanism. Therein he showed by most irrefragable proof that the uncompromising and relentless enemy of the progress of the United States is the so-called "Mother Country," because at no period in the history of this republic, whenever it was confronted by an overwhelming crisis, have we failed to meet her unsympathetic and relentless enmity. He repudiated the idea that England is the mother of the country and recognized that Europe is the parent which, from its loins, contributed the bone, the muscle and the brain of its best citizens and made us what we are. In exemplifying and emphasizing this fact Mr. Blaine incurred the enmity of a certain Anglomaniac faction that believe it is patriotic to glorify and magnify everything that comes from abroad and to discredit everything that is really American. His advocacy of the so-called "American System," his love for and belief in the merits and importance of the protective tariff brought upon him, when nominated for the important office of Chief Executive, the most virulent, malignant and abusive attacks that a private citizen was ever subjected to. These men invaded the tomb of the dead and the sanctuary of the living, in their malignant hate to destroy the man who more than any other in his person represented the unadulterated patriotism of those who believed in the permanency and supremacy of American institutions.

To an extent they succeeded, but I want to say here to-night that the fortunes of the battle of 1884 were decided by an insignificant five or six hundred votes in this great imperial State; yet, when you take into

consideration the fight that was made; the so-called
party organs that deserted the standard of the party;
the people who professed to be Republicans but who
separated themselves from the party and made the
fight on its candidate, I believe that the result was
the most magnificent personal triumph that was ever
accorded to any American citizen. The attack that
was made upon him was appalling, and yet his grand
personality stood out like the white plume of " Henry
of Navarre " as a standard around which every man
who believed in the principles of his party and the
patriotism of its candidate, felt he could rally without
fear of being deserted in the midst of strife or that
any retreat would ever be sounded.

Mr. President, let me call your attention to this fact,
that the most bitter of his attackers are already dead
and forgotten, and that in the course of time the rest
of those who joined in the same vile hunt and sought
to destroy him, will pass away and be buried in the
same grave of oblivion.

Blaine lives. He is not dead. His death was
but a step to eternity, in which he has become
immortal. When the men of generations to come
shall read the history of this country, they will
perceive that four names stand out like the stars in
the heavens — Washington, Jefferson, Hamilton and
Clay, as the men whose intelligence and genius gave
the formative principles to this republic; but in the
hour when its stability was to be tried, and the
capacity of democratic institutions for stable government tested, and they realize how successfully the
great crisis was met and overcome, among the long

roll of distinguished names that adorn that epoch in our national history, the ones that will fix their attention in supreme admiration and love will be Lincoln, Grant, Seward and Blaine. When the dirt flies that pursued him with rancour and hate shall have long been forgotten, the name of Blaine will be written upon every American heart with patriotic memories of his long and splendid services in behalf of his country, they will all be better Americans and more loyal supporters of free institutions, because of the example of his life.

So long as history records the deeds of men which make them great and their memory revered by a free people, there will be none in the bright galaxy of American citizens that will stand out more conspicuously or be remembered with greater reverence than the name of James G. Blaine.

By Senator McCarren :

Mr. President.— It is usual to say when men die that a void has been created. By the death of Mr. Blaine a character has been taken from our political life, a vacancy created that will remain unfilled. The particular place he occupied may be pointed out; his position may be reverted to, but there can be no substitution in the sense that the difference will not be apparent. The story of his life is only another verification of what many believe — that leaders are born and not made. Certainly, if the inherent possession of all those attributes that go to fit a man for the work of inspiring men to follow him, furnishes evidence of destiny, then Mr. Blaine's life proved the

---

affirmative side of that proposition. He lived in a period of our national life when opportunities were presented to our public men that seldom come in the history of a country. He left his impress on his time. He molded sentiment, he directed thought and he consummated events. It has been said that he failed in his ambition. Reasons have been and will be assigned for his failure. It is said of him he was fond of quoting the lines of that distinguished writer Nathaniel P. Willis, in which he asks and answers: "What is ambition? It is a glorious cheat. The angels of light do not walk so dazzlingly on the sapphired walls of heaven." If Mr. Blaine's life is to be measured from the standpoint of successful ambition it can be said that thus far American history is consistent in its record of shining marks of disappointment. It will always be admitted that Mr. Blaine did succeed in making his fame enduring. It will never be denied that his powers of oratory and his ability as a writer have earned for his memory a permanent place in American annals. The feeble tribute that I pay to his memory is induced by an admiration for his individuality. I had not even the honor of his personal acquaintance. His intimate friends can best speak of his genial temperament, his generous impulses and his warmth of heart. Everybody can speak of him as the typical American, as the man with the towering intellect, the versatility of talent, as the great civil captain. When he died a great man ceased to exist. His death, in my opinion, justifies the assertion that "the living are only the dead, the dead live never more to die."

In Memoriam.

By Senator EDWARDS:

MR. PRESIDENT.—Some one has compared our sorrow for the illustrious dead to a glorious sympathy with suns that set:

> "Even as the tenderness that hour instills,
> When summer's day declines along the hills,
> So feels the fullness of our heart and eyes
> When all of genius that can perish dies.
> A mighty spirit is eclipsed — a power
> Hath passed from day to darkness, to whose hour
> Of light, no likeness is bequeathed."

The death of James G. Blaine shadows a continent. His fame will endure. His name has already been chiseled upon the adamantine pillars of his country's history. He lived in a great, stirring epoch, and every part of that period felt the molding influence of his powerful hand. In writing his "Twenty Years in Congress," he might with Æneas, truly have said: "I chronicle that all of which I saw, and part of which I was." His powers of mind were amazingly versatile. He was distinguished as an orator, historian, statesman, diplomatist and political leader. His character was picturesque and striking, yet always massive and harmonious. He had a chieftain's boldness, with a sage's wisdom.

Those who looked upon only one side of his nature misunderstood him. Thus, when he became Secretary of State, there were those who feared that his brilliant and aspiring mind, and his aggressive Americanism, might plunge the country into foreign war. They thought him hot-headed and ambitious. But four times during his official career, he saved the country from perilous foreign complications by a happy blending of calmness, courage and firmness. Feel the iron grip of the gloved hand in his celebrated reply to Italy: "The United States has never yet permitted its policy to be dictated by any foreign power and it will not begin to do so now."

Nature often produces the grandest results by the operation of apparently opposite forces. It is sometimes thus with men. Those who saw Mr. Blaine, as a member of the House of Representatives or of the Senate, marshal his forces and lead them on to repeated victory, could think it scarce possible that he should become the historian of that very period, and perform his task in such a clean, judicial spirit that all would concede his estimates of men and measures to be distinguished by surpassing ability and perfect fairness.

The most conspicuous characteristic which appears in the career of Mr. Blaine is his Americanism. In behalf of all who sought our shores, as well as of the native born, he believed in conserving and advancing our own interests by binding together all the States of this western hemisphere, from Hudson bay to Patagonia, in friendly, commercial and industrial co-operation. He longed to see the ships of his country plowing the water of every harbor along the whole perimeter of our continent, and railroads binding together the remoter parallels of latitude.

Destiny did not deny to Mr. Blaine that supreme experience which has so often fallen to the lot of the great, and which has aided in giving them a pathetic and lasting remembrance among men. I mean tragic affliction. He was a man of sorrows. Again and again was he smitten by disappointment and by death.

In Memoriam.

The blows followed so rapidly that he had not staggered
up from one before another fell upon him. He might
have said, as did Edmund Burke at the climax of his
bereavements: "The storm has gone over me; I am
like one of the old oaks which the late hurricane has
scattered around us." Yet, amid it all there was no
unmanly complaining; no unkind, ungenerous word
fell from those eloquent lips. James G. Blaine had a
long memory for favors and a short one for offenses.
He was true and loving in his home. May Heaven
console his afflicted family, especially the companion
of his life, who was so utterly devoted to him.

Many have sought to find the key-note of his
character, especially for the purpose of explaining his
wonderful hold upon human hearts. Some have called
it personal magnetism; others, unflinching courage;
some patriotism, and others masterful intellectual
powers; but I shall call it manhood; manhood at its
best—true, gentle, sympathetic, tactful, capable, heroic,
chivalrous. In him men found noble ideals realized;
unfolded generously, attractively, and blended with the
persuasive, compelling force of a superb personality
which was born for leadership.

Like some others of the nation's greatest statesmen,
it was not his to enjoy the highest office in the gift
of the Republic; not his the ripe fruitions and happy
rewards of a peaceful old age; but over his grave
to-day men of all parties sincerely mourn, and they
frankly acknowledge, that there is left not one public
man, in all this broad land, who is his equal in varied
ability, nor one who is more firmly entrenched in the
hearts of his admiring countrymen.

James Gillespie Blaine.

By Mr. SMITH:

MR. PRESIDENT AND FELLOW SENATORS.—A great man, a prince among people, has ended his earthly career; a man rich in the many gifts with which God endowed him, who devoted himself for a generation to the service of his country and the people, winning the confidence and affection of all his countrymen, passes from us mourned, honored and loved.

James G. Blaine was great in statesmanship, leadership and in the field of literature, known not only in every household in our country, but to the statesmen of the civilized world; he was one of the illustrious characters which have demonstrated the value of free institutions. Nearly thirty of the sixty-three years of his life have been spent in public service, and the history of this nation during that time is to no small extent the history of his public life. During this long and eventful period he received the attention and commanded the respect of the people of this nation in a marked and unparalleled degree, unequaled unless in the cases of Lincoln and Clay. Like Clay, his followers were many, affectionate and enthusiastic, and like him he achieved great success, but failed to reach the goal of his ambition, the presidency. He was a remarkable man and wonderfully endowed. The country has produced no greater statesman or political leader, the ideal of his party, loved as no other man in it. By him was his party inspired more thoroughly than by any other. For many years he did more than any other leader to shape its policy. His tact in drawing men to him his control over them and ability to command their unselfish support was greater than that of any other party leader in the history of the country. His loss will be universally felt and mourned, but his life will continue to be an inspiration to his party.

One of the chief characteristics displayed by Mr. Blaine in diplomacy, as well as in every official act, was his exalted Americanism. A thorough believer in the Monroe doctrine and the reciprocity policy, which distinguished the close of his political career, will be conceded to be the outgrowth of his convictions respecting that doctrine. Of his political productions his diplomatic correspondence will rank as the best. Upon his acts as Secretary of State will mainly rest his reputation abroad, and it is not too much to say that during the past decade he has been the best known American in foreign lands. In our own country, the theater of his activity, his marvelous popularity, his loyalty to his country, to principles and friends, will be recognized by all. He was more truly a national leader than any man of our generation in civil life. Great must be the qualities of the man, who through so many strifes, covering so many years, both in public life and as a private citizen, holds the confidence and affections of the majority of his fellow men. It was in the House of Representatives that his readiness in debate, his knowledge of parliamentary law, his courage and skill had full and untrammeled sway. It was there he was more truly compared with Clay; it was there he won his spurs in his passage at words with Conkling, which cost him the Presidency. The controversy between these two masters of elocution, then young in congressional life, gave both a prominence in the nation, and planted seeds of enmity whose roots struck deep into the affairs of their party throughout the whole land. While many things transpired to deprive Mr. Blaine of the electoral vote of New York in 1884, and hence of the presidency, it is quite plain that but for the words spoken in that heated debate all things else would have failed to prevent his election. And while his failure to reach the presidential chair caused disappointment and regret to more people than would a like failure on the part of any other American citizen, yet he has by reason of such failure occupied positions where he could and has rendered services invaluable to his country; where his love for his country, its institutions and its flag has been clearly demonstrated; where he was able to and did prove that the welfare of his people and respect for his country's obligations were his highest concern.

He believed in protection because he realized that the first duty of a patriot and statesman is to care for the home. His genius and keen perceptions enabled him to see the value of reciprocity and against the inclinations of the executive, and in spite of the opposition of many party leaders he marshaled the forces of public opinion and it became law.

I hope no one will suppose Blaine reached his high position through luck or chance. Greatness does not come to men in some haphazard way; it comes as the result of industry, painstaking and toil. In youth he acquired these habits and carried them through life. In this as in many other things he has set an example to our people and youth worthy of imitation. From the high position he attained and the means he employed to attain it let the young men of our nation learn that the road to success does not lie along the path of negligence and idleness, a path' over which (it is to be regretted) so many of our youths are accustomed to travel, but it is to be found along the beaten path of honest toil and patient endurance.

If Blaine was a partisan he was a patriot as well. He did not love his party less but he loved his country more. Like him, if we use all our gifts to bring honor and success to our party; let it be because thus we desire and expect to benefit our country. Patisans we *may* be, patriots we *should* be. The greatest of America's statesmen and patriots, James G. Blaine, has fallen, but his works do follow him.

By Senator McClelland :

Mr. President.—It was not my purpose to have said anything to these resolutions to-night, but I think that I may call attention to the bitterness of the campaign of 1884 in which Mr. Blaine was a candidate for the highest office within the gift of the American people. If there ever was a time when the people should halt for a moment and reflect upon prevailing political methods it is now, when such resolutions are under consideration. It may be truly said, I think, that the army of admirers of James G. Blaine far exceeded the army of his followers. A host of American citizens who admired the character and works of James G. Blaine were not his followers because he was the leader and expounder of principles to which they could not subscribe; but what I meant to call attention to when I arose was the bitterness and the calumny of the campaign of 1884. I believe it may be truly said it never was excelled in the history of the American Republic. I have always opposed such methods in political warfare. Personal abuse, personal calumny, should have no place in a political campaign, and now I say that at this time the American people, and especially those who had any part in creating or disseminating this personal abuse, should reflect, and the American people should by every means possible put their stamp of condemnation upon such practices. It is after the lives of great men like James G. Blaine have closed and the chapter of their lives is complete, that we see what has been good in them; but should we not, Mr. President, if we have had any part or parcel in these intemperate tirades of abuse in utter disregard of the personal worth of these men, and the sacrifices made by them in their service to their country, if, I say, we have had any part or parcel in heaping that abuse, then it is to our personal dishonor, and we should blush for very shame. I trust that while all over the country similar resolutions are being passed in memory of this distinguished statesman, that the American people will think what a serious offense they have been guilty of to him at least.

The PRESIDENT put the question whether the Senate would agree to the above resolutions and they were unanimously adopted by a rising vote.

Then on motion of Mr. EDWARDS, the Senate adjourned out of respect to the memory of James G. Blaine.

PROCEEDINGS OF THE ASSEMBLY.

The Senate sent for concurrence a resolution in the words following :

Resolved (if the Assembly concur), That a joint committee, consisting of three Senators and five Members of Assembly, be appointed by the respective presiding officers of the two Houses for the purpose of presenting resolutions in memory of the deceased statesman James G. Blaine.

Mr. QUIGLEY moved the adoption of the concurrent resolution.

Mr. MALBY seconded the motion of Mr. Quigley, and the resolutions were adopted by a rising vote.

February 1, 1893.

Mr. SPEAKER announced the appointment of the following committee on the part of the House to prepare a memorial upon the late James G. Blaine : Messrs. Southworth, Hennessy, Morris, Terry and Diven.

A message from the Senate was received stating that the President of the Senate had appointed as a like committee on the part of the Senate, Messrs. Roesch, Bloodgood, and Saxton.

James Gillespie Blaine.

Mr. Southworth from the committee appointed to prepare a memorial on the death of Hon. James G. Blaine, presented the following:

Whereas, By the death of James Gillespie Blaine, this country has lost one of her most illustrious sons, a brilliant historian, an elegant orator, a matchless debater, an accomplished publicist, a great and renowned statesman, one whose genious has left an indelible impress for good upon our political life and national policies; one whose fame, leaping beyond the borders of his own land, has spread through all civilized nations; one who loved his country with the fervent love of the true patriot, and who-had a warmer place in the hearts of the American people than any other man of his time.

Resolved, That this Assembly give public expression to the profound sense of loss felt at this time by all classes of his fellow citizens in the Empire State; their gratitude for his priceless services; their sorrow for his death and respect for his memory.

Resolved, That these resolutions with the preamble be spread on the journal of the Assembly, and an engrossed copy of the same forwarded to his bereaved family, with the assurance of the deep sympathy felt for them by the individual members of this body.

Mr. Southworth, in moving the adoption of the foregoing resolutions, spoke as follows.

By Mr. Southworth:

Mr. Speaker.— In presenting for the consideration of the Legislature these resolutions from the committee, I desire briefly to add my testimony in appreciation of the loss which the country has sustained in the death of the distinguished gentleman whose memory the resolutions seek to preserve.

In the death of James G. Blaine, we lose one of the most conspicuous statesmen and one of the most remarkable men of modern times; conspicuous as a public leader, and remarkable for his learning and statesmanship.

Probably no public man of modern times provoked more vigorous opposition from the political party with which I have been associated, and certainly no one has been so earnestly and steadfastly supported by his own party.

To remember Mr. Blaine merely as a partisan, is to regard his memory in a narrow sense.

It is due to his public career that he should be remembered as having always kept in view the best interests of our common country, only employing party measures for the advancement of such interests.

To the Republican party belongs the honor of his leadership, but I, as a Democrat, admired his rock-ribbed republicanism and undaunted courage.

I love to think of a public man, who possessed the courage of his convictions, whose devotion to his party principles was so great as to prevent any wavering in his support, so firm as to preclude all idea of any abandonment of his party, even under the hottest fire of criticism of Democrats, or the mean detractions of those, who, disclaiming allegiance to any, seek to usurp the control of all parties.

The name of James G. Blaine will outlive all political parties. It has already become an important part of our country's history, and future generations will ever regard him as one who labored assiduously for the good of his country, holding his name in every American household as a synonym for patriotic citizen, good husband, kind and loving parent and honest man.

By Mr. QUIGLEY:

Mr. SPEAKER.— We are here to-night to do honor to the memory of a great man, a great American, a great historian and a great statesman. I will not take up the time of the House with any extended remarks on the resolutions. There are others who will follow me who are better able to do justice to the subject; but I wish to say that the heart of the nation mourns the loss of a great man whose life was an example of the possibilities that lie in the path of American citizenship. Loved and honored by his neighbors, great in his party, respected by his political opponents, powerful and influential in the halls of the Congress of the nation, he has left an indelible page in the history of our country. A history that he was part of, a history that he contributed to.

James G. Blaine was a great historian and his "Twenty Years in Congress" is a complete and impartial history of the times. For this impartial and fair history, treating North and South with equal fairness, he will be remembered as one of the historians of the generation.

While the Republican party may mourn its loss, the citizens of this nation, of whatever party, join in paying honor to his memory, because he deserves honor. Mr. Blaine's life was an example for our young men who are ambitious to shine in our politics. His death was a nation's loss.

In Memoriam.

By Mr. MALBY:

Mr. SPEAKER. — James Gillespie Blaine, America's greatest statesman and the idol of the people, is dead.

> " He did not fall like drooping flowers, which no man noticeth,
> But, like a great branch of some stately tree
> Rent in tempest and flung down to death,
> Thick with green leafage, so that piteously
> Each passer-by that ruin shuddereth
> And saith: The gap this breach hath left is wide,
> The loss thereof can never be supplied."

In the midst of darkness there is light, and as we mourn the loss of our distinguished leader, the hard lines are softened by words of praise and commendation of his life and doings by those who have opposed his principles during the past quarter of a century. It is a peculiar and striking characteristic of the American people, that they may differ never so widely as to policies, but when one of those who advocate them shall pass away, his opponents have the manliness to acknowledge his greatness and ability, according to the work which he has performed.

" Death holds a flag of truce over its own. Under that flag friend and foe sit peacefully together, passions are stilled, benevolence is restored, wrongs are repaired, justice is done."

History informs us that the deceased statesman was born about sixty-two years ago in a little country town in the old State of Pennsylvania. Born of good old revolutionary stock, and gifted with a strong constitution, a noble character and a superior mind. He was a self-made man.

James Gillespie Blaine.

In his youth, the usual necessaries of a country life were furnished him, but he had no luxuries. At the age of thirteen he entered college, and at seventeen graduated with high honors. The years that followed which he spent as teacher, law student and editor, are full of interest. As teacher, it was said of him that "His brilliant mental powers were exactly qualified to enlighten and instruct the interesting minds before him." In the study of law, he became familiar with statutes, legislative proceedings and international and diplomatic relations, and it was then he laid the foundation in legal principles which made him an eminent and world-wide authority along these lines of jurisprudence. As editor of the Kennebec Journal, he became a power in State politics. His editorials were able and vigorous, and made him at once the leader of his party in the Pine Tree State.

The first elective honor conferred upon him, was his election as a delegate to the First Republican National Convention, and which nominated John C. Fremont for President. To those on this side of the house, we are proud to say, that he assisted in rocking the cradle of republicanism.

Shortly thereafter we find him a member of the State Legislature of his adopted State, where he continued three years, the last two as its honored Speaker. It is probable that while occupying this position, he became familiar with parliamentary law and with the manner of dealing with men, and familiarized himself with great public subjects, which afterwards enabled him to become the leader in national affairs.

In Memoriam.

The people who knew him best appreciated his abilities, and in 1862, elected him to Congress, where he served in one branch or the other for eighteen years. He was there during the trying ordeals of war, and with voice and word he said, "The nation must be preserved, and whatever is necessary to be done to put down this war, whatever resources are required by those in charge of the government, we must freely give unto them." And to his masterly aid, we, to-day, owe much for a reunited country, and that the principles of civil and religious liberty still survive.

After the war was over, and the union had been preserved, he assisted, I think, more than any other man in bringing the seceded States back into the union as they ought to come. Their desire was to return of their own motion, and according to such terms and provisions as they themselves might prescribe, but Mr. Blaine said "No. You must adopt the fourteenth amendment; you must guarantee to every citizen the right of suffrage; you must petition the Congress of the United States for admission, and if they say, well done, then you return, but until that time you are not one of us."

The fourteenth amendment embodied Mr. Blaine's proposition, which was submitted by himself, and largely through his exertions was finally adopted.

In 1869, so distinguished had become his services, so grand and fearless his leadership, that his party unanimously nominated him as Speaker of the House of Representatives, and for three successive terms he received the unanimous nomination of his party, an honor, which, in the history of our country for more than a century, has never been accorded to any other man. Probably this country has never produced so able a presiding officer of the House of Representatives. The brilliancy of this period of his career has been attributed to his "real aptitude and equipment for the duties of a presiding officer; and his complete mastery of parliamentary law, his dexterity and physical endurance, his rapid dispatch of business, and his firm and impartial spirit."

His abilities as presiding officer will ever be recognized by all those who come hereafter, and I think it was then he performed the most distinguished services of his early life. He wielded a mighty power; he was the absolute master of national politics at that time. The legislation which was placed upon our statute books was largely due to his masterly genius, his great and originative mind.

> "Wherever the bright sun of Heaven shall shine,
> His honor and the greatness of his name shall be."

In the year 1874, the party of Blaine found themselves in a minority of the Lower House of Congress, and Mr. Blaine returned to the floor, where as leader of the minority he engaged in all the tilts of that tempestuous session; and in no other position did he acquit himself better. He always possessed the courage of his convictions, and the absolute confidence of his associates.

> "In halls of State he stood for many years,
> Like fabled knight, his visage all aglow,
> Receiving, giving sternly, blow for blow.
> Champion of right."

In 1876 Mr. Blaine took his seat in the Senate of the United States, the greatest legislative body, I think, in the world I do not believe that Mr. Blaine was at home there. The more turbulent body, the Lower

House, was the place for which he was better fitted, naturally, than a conservative body like the Senate of the United States; but even there he was prominent in debate, and the statute books of that time bear evidence of his great ability, his research and his industry.

In 1876 he was a candidate for the nomination to the presidency of the United States. Long and serious was the contest in the Republican National Convention, which finally resulted in the nomination of another, but Mr. Blaine, firm to the principles of his party, and strong in his Americanism, supported the nominee with all his influence and with all the mighty power he possessed.

History soon repeated itself, for in 1880 Mr. Blaine was again a candidate and again another was nominated, and again he led his party to victory. In 1884, his aspirations to become the candidate of his party were fulfilled. He was nominated at a time, however, when our party was rent asunder. Internal dissensions had made it almost impossible to nominate anybody with any assurances of an election. The only name which suggested itself to the American people at that time as at all fit for the coming contest was the great statesman from Maine. He was nominated, and immediately the opposition newspapers ran full of vituperation which increased in volume as the campaign continued.

> " No might or greatness in mortality
> Can censure 'scape; back wounding calumny
> The whitest virtue strikes. What king so strong
> Can tie the gall up in the slanderous tongue ? "

James Gillespie Blaine.

Mr Blaine had an abiding faith in the honesty of the American people, and they trusted him. He stood up under the terrible ordeal, and success seemed assured, until an erratic person in the city of New York, representing no one but himself, uttered three words, which were immediately sent broadcast throughout our country, to every State, every city, every town and every home. It had its effect, and Blaine was cheated out of the presidency. Our greatest statesman of modern times, and the idol of the people retired to private life. He gave to the world, perhaps, more by his defeat than he would had his efforts been crowned with success, for in his retirement he wrote that admirable work, his " Twenty Years in Congress."

His style was strong, vigorous and incisive, and it stands as an enduring monument to his intellectual faculties, his impartiality and his broad statesmanship.

In 1888 he was still the leader of his party, and loved by the people, and would again have been nominated, but he absolutely refused. A letter came from Florence and from Paris and a telegram from Edinburgh, stopping the American people from doing that which they seemed bound to do. It was only after he had dropped into the convention a telegram absolutely refusing to accept the nomination that our party's representatives in convention assembled, concluded to respect his wishes. Though not a candidate, he framed the issues of that campaign, which led his party triumphantly to success.

I would speak for a moment of those distinguished services he rendered as Secretary of State when he first entered the cabinet of President Garfield. It was charged that he was a reckless statesman, and that he would cause trouble and war to come upon our country; that his ambition would not be satisfied with the usual and ordinary discharge of public duties; but time has demonstrated the injustice of this charge. He made a grand Secretary of State, and when the assassin's bullet shot down the leader of our republic, he, faithful in all things, remained true to his chief and his country, practically conducted the government, and discharged the duties of President until death relieved our suffering President.

As Secretary of State in President Harrison's Cabinet, his services have been still more distinguished. I think that it has never been allotted to a man in his position to do more.

The controversy with Chili was on our hands; the Samoan controversy with Germany troubled him; the British government claimed to have certain rights in the Northern Pacific, and the Italian difficulties at New Orleans also claimed his attention, but in the discharge of his duties as Secretary of State, he was fully equal to all emergencies, and all but one have been settled to the satisfaction and honor of the United States, and the other is in a fair way of a like solution.

Nor did he encourage war, but instead formulated a policy which will prevent war, at least in the Western Hemisphere against the United States for all time to come. He called together the representatives of all nations on this side of the Atlantic in the Pan-American Congress, and they consulted together, and his scheme of reciprocity was at that time suggested and since largely adopted, and by which every mechanic, every laborer and every farmer in the whole country has received and will continue to receive benefits.

But, Mr. Speaker, to enumerate all the great events in our national history, in which he acted a leading part, would require more time than propriety would here allow. Let it suffice to state that as he drew near the end of a life so actively engaged in the greatest deeds and greatest problems which have interested the statesmen of any time, this great son of our republic, diseased in body and weary in mind, laid down his high office and retired to his home, among his neighbors and friends. He retired to the ever sounding sea in search of health, in search of rest, but it was not to be found. Long suffering, he returned to the scenes of his active life, hoping there perhaps, to escape the consequences of the dreaded disease which was sapping his life and vitality away. Week after week, his sufferings continued, and a great nation inquired from day to day and from hour to hour, "How he was," but as the days of men are numbered, so it was with him. The time came when in humble submission to the divine decree, he took a loving leave of his faithful wife, devoted children and admiring friends, bravely and fearlessly, full of hope, sustained by faith he passed from this life to death and from death to the dawn of an eternal morning. Of him it may with truth be said —

> "Oh death, where is thy sting!
>   Oh grave, where is thy victory!"

> "From eternity's far shore
>   Thy spirit will return to join no more.
>   Rest citizen, statesman, rest;
>   Thy troubled life is o'er."

By Mr. Martin:

If I might be permitted, I desire to say a few words upon the resolutions just presented. The death of James

In Memoriam.

G. Blaine has removed from our public life one of its most conspicuous members. In the length of his public service, in the versatility of his talents, in the brilliancy of the results which he accomplished, he has equaled the most distinguished statesmen who have achieved prominence in the history of our land.

Few men of mark have been idolized by the American people as James G. Blaine has been. He had a warm and impetuous nature, a vigorous and well-trained mind, and a magnetism of individuality which irresistibly attracted, and ultimately wore itself out in the surging and rapid tide of public life.

He is, Mr. Speaker, a public example of the possibilities of American citizenship. With no unusual advantages in his youth, he grasped every opportunity that was presented; and went from one avocation to another, with such persistent determination, that honor and glory were the final rewards of his efforts.

In his early manhood, he was elected Speaker of the House of Representatives; and he gained for himself the reputation of having been one of the best presiding officers that body has ever had. As United States Senator he added to the reputation thus acquired; and as Secretary of State he maintained the dignity and supremacy of this nation in all matters of international moment affecting the interests of the western world.

His capacity was discovered in his ripening years. Impulse waited on reflection and experience leavened a nature that had been but too sensitive and sympathetic. Responsibility, disappointment and sorrow did not lessen his ambition nor weaken his energies; they had but mellowed his heart and ripened his mind.

In the seventies he was merely a shrewd politician; in the nineties he was a broad statesman. Cultured beyond the plane of modern public men, yet was he more in touch with the thought and aspirations of his fellow citizens than men more intimately associated with them in their daily walks of life. He had the prescient vision of a prophet, and saw that these United States were no longer the frontier of European civilization. The Monroe doctrine was an imperative necessity, dictated by wise and prudent statesmanship. We were few and feeble, and desired to be permitted to grow in strength and numbers. Our limitations precluded an interference with other nations. To-day we have outgrown the environment of old policies and inland prejudices.

In population, commerce, wealth and magnitude we equal the proudest nations of the earth. And the health, prosperity and peace of other nations are of the utmost import to our own. Blaine recognized these conditions and made them the basis of his international policy. He believed in a protective tariff but not in an exclusive one. He foresaw that a wider market was imperatively needed, and his formulation of the policy of reciprocity was the result. As Secretary of State his enemies believed he would inaugurate a policy of brag and bluster. But they were deceived. His diplomatic negotiation of difficult cases was pacific and dignified. It is generally conceded that the Chilian affair would have terminated

more successfully had the Harrison administration
refrained from interfering.

The Behring Sea matter was wisely transferred to
a board of arbitration, and the New Orleans assas-
sinations were settled in a delicate and honorable
manner. Blaine was intensely American, for he
dearly loved the welfare and glory of his native
land.

And yet, Mr. Speaker, whether he shall be remembered as a writer or an orator, a politician or a
statesman, his personality has been so closely and so
intimately woven into the very fabric of our land,
that the history of this country will be incomplete
and insufficient if the name of Blaine be omitted
from its pages.

Like Clay and Webster, he unsuccessfully aspired
to the presidency of the United States; and like
unto them, also, he will go down to meet the coming
ages as the most distinguished statesman of his time,
and as the glorious epitome of the age in which he
lived.

I second the motion, that the resolutions be adopted.

By Mr. AINSWORTH :

Mr. SPEAKER.— It rarely falls to the lot of any man
to do as much for the cause of human progress, as it
has to the man in honor of whose memory these
proceedings are being held.

James G. Blaine has impressed his personality upon
the time in which he lived to a greater extent than
any other American citizen, in times of peace, during
the history of our country.

James Gillespie Blaine.

As a teacher, as an editor, as a politician, in the broadest sense of that term, for twenty years the chairman of the State committee of the party to which he belonged in his native State, for fourteen years a Member of Congress, for six years the presiding officer of that body, twice a United States Senator, four times a candidate in National Convention for the office of chief magistrate of this nation, once a candidate before the people for that great office, twice Secretary of State of the United States, and as the author of the greatest work upon political economy that the age has produced, he was in all these capacities a conspicuous success, and in many of them complete master of the situation.

The versatility of his mind, as evidenced by the wide range of subjects mastered, is phenomenal.

As I have reviewed his career, Mr. Speaker, I have tried to discover in what it was that he excelled, and what was the faculty that won for him the love and admiration of the American people; and when I view his character through all these many years of public life and see the magnificent success that has crowned all his efforts, I think it was his distinctive Americanism emphasized in every public act, that won for him the confidence and esteem of the people in a degree possessed by no other American.

We all believe now that the flag of the United States should protect every citizen of our native land, native or foreign born, at home or abroad; and yet it was the voice of Blaine that first directed attention to that principle, when on the floor of the United States Congress he said to England in language afterwards adopted by Congress, "You must reverse your policy of centuries of growth, crystallized in the national enunciation — 'once a citizen always a citizen' — and you must put in its place that broader American principle, that the native and the naturalized citizen of the United States shall be protected by her flag wherever it floats."

When Costello and Warren and Burke, naturalized citizens of the United States, were incarcerated in British prisons, it was the Americanism of James G. Blaine that forced this nation to proclaim to England "our flag protects these men, naturalized citizens, as it would had they been on our shores."

When the commercial interests of our people were demanding wider markets for American products, it was the Americanism of James G. Blaine that conceived the policy of uniting all of the American Republics in a commercial union, whose interests should center around the United States, and which will ultimately make this country the clearing house for the Western Hemisphere; and to-day every avenue of business feels the quickening inspiration that came from that thought of James G. Blaine.

We all remember in 1887 when that message of President Cleveland's invoking a new departure in the economic administration of this government was sent out, how politicians of our country, the editors of our great newspapers, uniformly so keen in detecting and utilizing every great opportunity, practically passed it by, until there flashed from old Rome where James G. Blaine was enjoying

James Gillespie Blaine.

his well earned vacation in cessation from public duties an answer to the proposition thus advanced, and his intense Americanism asserted itself in the reply that was wired to this country and which by unanimous consent immediately became the platform upon which the magnificent victory of 1888 was won by his party.

When vast numbers of our people sought to pay the debts of our government by the creation of other debts and new paper promises, his was one of the first voices raised to sound the alarm and he was largely instrumental in establishing the only honest and patriotic principle that the gold of the realm, pledged by national honor in time of distress should be the only payment recognized by us in settlement of our debts.

I know that he has been censured. The Press of our country in his day winged at him the poisoned arrows of criticism, with the venom characteristic of the age. In a lesser degree they did at Washington, Lincoln and Garfield.

But to-day a great nation stands uncovered in the presence of death, recognizing that in his demise we suffer a national loss, and by its reverent sorrow stamps the criticism as cruel and unjust.

It has always been that greatest scandal waits on greatest state.

>The crow can dip its coal-black wings in mire
>And, undiscovered, fly with its filth away;
>But should the like the snow white swan desire.
>The stain upon its silver down would stay.

In Memoriam.

When the history of his time shall have been fully written, the criticism so prominent during the most active years of his life will remain unrecorded, while his intense Americanism, his breadth of thought, his intense devotion to the interests of his country, will place him with Lincoln and Bismarck and Gladstone, as the greatest men of his age.

By Mr. O'Sullivan:

We have turned from the common course of our deliberations for a moment to consider an event in the history of the world; and the manner of our turning, no less than the cause of it, awakens reflections which lead us a long way back in the path of history — back to those chivalrous times when plumed knights on tented fields sought death or glory in defense of the colors they wore; back to those times when mailed barons, sword in hand, defended their castles against the encroachments of invading barons. Through the obscurity which bedims the history of those distant times we can catch the gleam of many a wholesome and beautiful custom, but of none more wholesome or beautiful than that mediæval custom called the "Truce of God." When the vesper bell had sounded the knell of departing day, as though a better world conversed with ours, all conflict between man and man was ceased. Even though the sword had pierced through links of steel on its way to the warrior's breast when the evening chime had sounded the knell of departing day, as though heaven itself had spoken, the sword found its scabbard, and warrior's hand sought warrior's hand in the grasp of peace.

James Gillespie Blaine.

To-night we, of opposing political creeds, believe that no warrior of old ever contended for nobler colors than those for the security of which we contend — the colors which stand for American freedom, the flag of our country.

We believe that no men of any clime or time ever defended homes more dear to them than are ours to us — the homes upon which the nation itself is founded. Representing these homes here, but regarding their security through conflicting political views, we sometimes meet in the clash of political conflict. In the heat of debate we may sometimes forget the sincerity of purpose which animates opposition to us, and forgetfulness may lead to bitter animosity; but now we banish all bitterness and political dissension. Strife is changed to peace, because heaven has spoken again, and this time James Gillespie Blaine has answered its call. Well may we meet in peace this hour, and profitably may we devote ourselves to the memory of that grand American whose bark is now sailing out on Eternity's Sea, because the principles which we cherish and the homes that we love have lost a friend in the death of James Gillespie Blaine. Thousands of his countrymen have lost the idol of their lives, his party a Warwick, and his country a citizen who, above all things, was American, grandly American to the last.

But the Americanism of Blaine was not confined by the boundaries of his country; it spread out over this entire western continent; it spread out over this entire western world, from the ice-bound fields of the North to the surging seas of the South. When future generations shall behold all the nations of these American continents in the full enjoyment of that peace, that prosperity, and that freedom which we now enjoy, then shall they behold realized the hopeful Americanism of James Gillespie Blaine.

Kind and gentle as a child, bold and daring as a lion, he was loved by his friends and feared by his foes. Believing that there was no place in American politics for the flying squadrons of political fortune hunters, he was deeply partisan. His zealous partisanship, his brilliant mind, and the charm of his eloquence were devoted to the development and the success of his party to such an extent that his party's losses and his party's triumphs were largely the losses and the triumphs of Blaine

A writer and maker of history, he left little else to the political historian of his time than the story of Blaine.

Not only the parties and the history of his time felt the influence of his power; but he even left the impression of his genius upon the Constitution of his country; so that his name shall not die while the Union lives; and the Union shall live and go on to the accomplishment of its magnificent destinies, while American citizens, regardless of political affiliations unite in tributes of devotion to the memory of such an American as James Gillespie Blaine.

I second the resolution.

By Mr. R. HOBBIE:

Mr. SPEAKER.—I trust I shall not be considered guilty of impropriety in presuming to add a word to the

---

eloquent tributes that have been paid to the memory of the illustrious dead. As a native of that State which he particularly loved, and which has been identified with his public life for more than a quarter of a century. I have watched with glad pride his uninterrupted advance through the various gradations of national distinction, until he stood alone before the world the acknowledged leader of his time. And I feel, sir, that that State and her citizens have sustained a loss which benumbs all power of expression. There are griefs which lie too deep for words. And yet the grief of her sons is not an isolated sorrow. Their bereavement is shared by the citizens of this imperial commonwealth, which has felt not only the strong pulsation of the channels of commerce responding to the impress of his far-seeing, beneficent public policy but has also experienced the thrill of patriotic fervor when, at his command, the bonds of foreign prisons were burst asunder, and an astonished world learned that no bolts nor bars were strong enough to hold, for a moment unoffending American citizens — aye, citizens of our own Empire State — acknowledging their allegiance to the land of their birth or adoption. In the observance of this hour Maine and New York but voice the swelling tide of sorrow which rolls across the continent; no American so humble but feels a personal loss, none so exalted but mourns his great leader gone. My heart has been deeply moved by the vivid portrayal of the events of his life, the eloquent recital of his distinguished public services, his wisdom, candor and courage, the impressive appeal to the intelligent manhood of America to emulate and perpetuate his illustrious example, and, sir, as an American, who realizes the

supreme dignity conferred upon American citizenship
by the intensity of his enlightened patriotism, I have
felt constrained to acknowledge, however imperfectly,
my own sense of gratitude to him who will stand forth
among the historic figures of this century as the pre-
eminent exponent of American ideas, aims and civilization — JAMES GILLESPIE BLAINE.

By Mr. TERRY:

MR. SPEAKER.— Another soul, restless in human sphere,
has broken the chains that bound it to mortality. The
light of another life has gone out forever. Again the
funeral train, with measured tread, has borne its
burden to the tomb. Again the nation mourns. And
here to-night, pausing at the grave of the distinguished dead, I, too, bow in reverence and drop a tear
of sorrow for his untimely death.

I can not add to what has already been said in review
of the life-history of the deceased, nor to the eulogies,
eloquent and fitting, that have been pronounced upon
him by the honorable gentlemen who have preceded
me, and yet, in memory of a life spent in the service
of his country and sacrificed upon its altar, in appreciation of human merit and excellence, in homage to
intellectual power and greatness, in adoration of James
Gillespie Blaine, I desire to say a word on this solemn
occasion.

During the darkest days in the history of our
country, when unholy war was the arbitrator between
the North and the South, and later, when the great
problems of reconstruction were the absorbing topics
of national consideration, it frequently was my privilege

and pleasure to listen to Mr. Blaine in debate, in the House of Congress. It was there I became acquainted with him; it was there I learned to respect and admire him, and ever since, during the many years that have followed, I have watched his advance, step by step, to honor and fame. The way was steep and rugged, with pitfalls on every hand; but fearlessly walking in the light of those memorable words of his early manhood, "Dare to do right, and trust the consequences to Infinite Wisdom," he overcame every obstacle and proudly strode onward and upward to the exalted position of America's greatest statesman.

Such lofty eminence, with its honors and rewards, its powers and privileges, could not escape the attacks of bitter jealousy. Had he enemies? Many of them, to his credit be it said. Who has not, who has the courage of his convictions, or whose independence of thought and action is worthy of example? Disappointed ambition hesitates not to assail the honored, nor men of inferior intellects, to disparage mental and moral greatness. Always in the advance in formulating great measures of national interest, and undaunted in his advocacy of them, it is not strange that sometimes his motives were criticised and his theories condemned; but the lapse of time, with its opportunities for the fulfillment of his plans, demonstrated the purity of his intentions, the genius of his mind and the wisdom of his policies. A partisan, ambitious and zealous, he may have been, but that which men denounce to-day as partisanship ofttimes to-morrow is patriotism. Whether surrounded by the cares and perplexities of official position, or in social or private life, he was

the same courteous, genial and polished gentleman.
In presence he was dignified, majestic; tireless in
action, eloquent in speech and peerless in debate.

But, alas, with the zenith of fame still in the dis-
tance; with his fondest life-hope crushed to earth;
with the years allotted man to live not yet numbered
to him; perchance with other and greater measures of
national greatness awaiting discovery in his master
mind, DEATH, that mysterious something of which we
have neither knowledge nor understanding, overtook
him and bore him to the silent halls of the dead.

"Dust to dust, ashes to ashes"—how solemn and
cheerless the words—and the grave closed 'round him
forever. Is that all?—the end of all? Does he sleep
the sleep that knows no waking, or shall he in the
fullness of time put on immortality? "As the cloud
is consumed and vanisheth away, so he that goeth
down to the grave shall come up no more," saith
the Prophet. Can this be? Then dark and hopeless
indeed is the future. But not so: within every heart
a voice whispers of the resurrection morn, of eternal
life, of happy reunions and holy associations beyond
the veil in the Kingdom of God. With these
assurances and believing, as we may, that not only
he whose loss we lament to-night but the dead of
all the ages past, our own loved ones as well, are
waiting for us, yea, are beckoning us from the other
shore, verily the sting, the mockery of death is
shorn of bitterness.

He can not come up to us but we shall go down to
him. The way of life, strewn with cares and hedged
with anguish, is but a span long; the cradle and

the grave follow in quick succession; and time, like a stream in narrow gorge, rushes on in headlong haste to the eternity of years—to that haven of peace "where the wicked cease from troubling and the weary are at rest."

> "A wonderful stream is the river of time,
>   As it runs through the realm of tears;
>   With a faultless rhythm and a musical rhyme,
>   And a broader sweep and a surge sublime,
>   As it blends in the ocean of years."

Pyramids of granite, beautiful in design and appropriate in inscription, will testify a people's tribute to his worth; but these, with the burden of centuries upon them, may crumble to dust. Not so the monuments of his own creation — his public and private life. These, ages shall not efface nor time destroy but as "as a cloud by day and a pillar of fire by night," they shall endure forever to inspire the youth of our land to nobler aims, to loftier ambitions, to lives of honor and renown.

Mr. Speaker, a mighty man has fallen; a noble chieftain, an eminent statesman has gone to his rest. We mourn, we offer kind words of sympathy to the afflicted family and friends; but, considering that which most concerneth him, let us dry our tears, for our loss is his gain.

By Mr. McCormick:

Mr. Speaker.—The county of Orleans stands second to no other in its admiration for the distinguished services and great ability of the honored dead; and it desires upon this occasion to join hands with the other counties of this great State in doing honor to the life and character of James G. Blaine, and in rendering proper sympathy to his family and his friends. The vocabulary of adjectives has already been exhausted, which are proper to be used on this occasion, by the distinguished gentlemen who have preceded me; and, Mr. Speaker, as I have no desire to hold this House to listen to a repetition of the same, I will, at once, in behalf of the county which I have the honor to represent, most heartily and sincerely second the motion for the adoption of the resolutions.

Mr. SPEAKER put the question whether the House would agree to the adoption of the foregoing resolutions, and they were adopted unanimously.

Then, on motion of Mr. Quigley, the House adjourned.